THIS BLOOMSBURY BOOK
BELONGS TO

....

To Catherine and Jack, with love from Mummy
L.M.

To my lovely jubbly niece Evie. x
M.B.

Bloomsbury Publishing, London, Berlin and New York

First published in Great Britain in 2009 by Bloomsbury Publishing Plc
36 Soho Square, London, W1D 3QY

Text copyright © Liz Martinez 2009
Illustrations copyright © Mark Beech 2009
The moral rights of the author and illustrator have been asserted

A CIP catalogue record of this book is available from the British Library

ISBN 978 0 7475 9702 5

Printed in China

1 3 5 7 9 10 8 6 4 2

All papers used by Bloomsbury Publishing are natural, recyclable products made
from wood grown in well-managed forests. The manufacturing processes conform
to the environmental regulations of the country of origin

www.bloomsbury.com/childrens

The EVERYDAY Witch

Liz Martinez and Mark Beech

BLOOMSBURY

LONDON BERLIN NEW YORK

This is a story for people who think
That witches, these days, are completely extinct,
When an Everyday Witch might be living next door . . .

Regular Housewife

A regular
housewife
and mother
of four.

Aunty Maude

She might be
your auntie

Chum

or even your chum.

But how would you feel
if she was **your mum?**

'Are you a witch, Mum?'
asked Jimmy one day.
'Never you mind, love,'
was all she would say.

Jimmy was worried.

He'd recently learned

That his mother was possibly

one who had

'turned'.

So on Saturday, late, when he should be in bed,

Jimmy drew back the curtains a little instead.

He peered through the darkness then leapt back in fright

As a witch on a broomstick

zoomed past in the night.

Jimmy froze in his slippers a second or two,

feeling very confused.
Well, what would you do,

If a **witch** on a broom flew by,
under your nose,

Waved
at you,
winked
at you,

**struck a
cool pose,**

In pink stripy stockings,
a big pointy hat,

And sitting behind her
**was Tiddles,
your cat?**

The following morning he lay wide awake,
Desperately hoping he'd made some mistake.

Was his mother a witch?

Could it really be true?

He needed more proof,

a definitive clue.

He'd heard about witches from stories in books,
But could you be sure just from somebody's looks?

It's useless, he thought, I need tips on detection.
So he went to the library and looked through the section
Of books about **witches** and folk of the night.
But none of them said how to spot one by sight.

Then, at last, in a second-hand bookshop he found
The smallest of books, in black leather bound:
Identify Witches (not just by their kit) –
In Q and A format. **At last, this was it!**

That night, by torchlight, when tucked up in bed,
He opened the book to find out what it said:
Simply answer these questions with NO or with YES.
Your answers will show you a true sorceress.

Does she wear stripy stockings, a pointy black hat?

Does she have a long broomstick, a black witchy cat?

Is she terribly ugly with warts on her nose,
And a horrible smell from her musty old clothes?
Does she brew putrid potions
which smoke in the pot?

Does she howl like a banshee
and cackle a lot?

frogs eyes

Newt legs

Does she cultivate potent medicinal herbs
Which she uses in poultices, brews and preserves?

The questions were endless and very precise.

They certainly didn't make **witches** sound nice.

The more Jimmy read, the more he felt numb.

Could any of this stuff apply to his mum?

She'd once had a wart –
is that really a clue?
If it was,
then my best friend
could be a witch too!

She does have a rather
large cookery pot,

And dabbles with strange herbs like bergamot.

She makes her own medicines, prefers them to pills,

Says that a doctor can't cure all ills

(though they taste quite disgusting and some really sting,

Mum says that they're natural and cure everything).

Our cat's black, it's true, but old Tiddles is shy.

I don't think she'd like
being up in the sky.

Soon Jimmy decided
he'd read quite enough.

'I must have been dreaming.
It's nonsense, this stuff!'

tansy

toad bladder

Bat wings

Snail Snot

As the weeks passed he laughed that he'd been such a fool

... Until one fateful day when he came home from school.

As he walked up the path, there they were on the line ...

Stripy stockings,

a black gown –

the ultimate sign!

St John's Wort.

She believes love can heal with a power that's divine,
So she kisses you better to make you feel fine.
Her magic is ancient, her wisdom's not new;
It was used by her mother and grandmother too.

But throughout history it has been misunderstood.
It is totally natural, all for the good.'
Despite reeling a bit from this swift education,
Jimmy felt reassured by his mum's explanation.

His mother's a witch,
and a wonderful mum.
She likes life to be magical.
So does her son.

. . . Unless, of course, the moon is bright
And it's a starry, spooky kind of night.
If you'd rather not see your mum posing mid-flight,

Keep your curtains drawn and your eyes
shut
tight!